This Ladybird Book belongs to:

This Ladybird retelling
by
Audrey Daly

Ladybird books are widely available, but in case of difficulty may be ordered by post or telephone from:

Ladybird Books – Cash Sales Department
Littlegate Road Paignton Devon TQ3 3BE
Telephone 0803 554761

A catalogue record for this book is available from the British Library

Published by Ladybird Books Ltd Loughborough Leicestershire UK
Ladybird Books Inc Auburn Maine 04210 USA

Printed in EC

FAVOURITE TALES

Beauty and the Beast

illustrated
by
ROBERT AYTON

based on a traditional French fairy tale

Once, long ago, a rich merchant lost his whole fortune. All he had left was a little house in the country, and he went there to live, taking his three daughters with him.

The two elder daughters were angry at having to live in the country, and they did nothing but complain all day.

But the youngest daughter cheerfully looked after the house and helped her father in his vegetable garden.

She was her father's favourite, and he called her Beauty.

One day the merchant had to go away on business.

"Are there any special presents you would like me to bring back?" he asked his daughters.

The older sisters both asked for precious jewels, but Beauty just smiled and said,"I should love to have some white roses."

The merchant promised to bring each of them what they had asked for.

The merchant’s business did not take long, and he was soon on his way home. But when darkness fell, he lost his way in the forest.

Before long he came to a palace. As he drew near to it, he saw that the door was open.

After making sure his horse had food and shelter, the merchant went inside. No one seemed to be there, but he found a table set with a splendid feast.

The merchant waited to see if anyone came. No one did, so he ate every scrap of food.

Afterwards, he found a comfortable bedroom, where he went to sleep.

Next morning, to his surprise, the merchant found a new suit in place of his own. He put it on and went to the room where he had eaten the night before.

Breakfast was waiting for him. “I can hardly believe my good fortune,” he said to himself as he ate.

As the merchant set off to get his horse, he saw some white rose bushes and remembered his promise to Beauty.

Just as he was about to pick a rose, a furious voice cried, "Those are *my* roses!" The merchant turned to see a huge, ferocious-looking Beast glaring at him.

"I gave you food, and a bed, and new clothes," bellowed the Beast. "Now you steal my roses as well! For that, you shall die!"

The merchant shook with fear. “Please don’t kill me,” he begged. “The roses are for my daughter.”

The Beast had little pity, but he looked thoughtfully at the merchant. Then he said, “Only one thing can save you. You must promise to return in a month's time, bringing with you the first living thing to meet you when you get home."

The terrified merchant had to agree.

The merchant quickly found his way home. At first, as he rode, he was just happy to be free.

Then he began to wonder who or what would be first to greet him – would it be his cat, or his dog? Then a terrible thought came to him – it might be Beauty!

And of course, it was.

When the merchant sadly told his daughter of his promise, Beauty said that such a promise must be kept.

So when four short weeks had passed, the merchant rode back to the palace with a heavy heart. In his arms he held his favourite daughter.

At the palace, a table was set and waiting for them. But Beauty and her father were too unhappy to eat.

Suddenly they heard heavy footsteps, and the Beast strode in. “Is this the daughter who likes white roses?” he asked gruffly.

"Yes," said the merchant. "She made me keep my promise to you."

"I shall not harm her," said the Beast gently. "But you must leave now."

Beauty wept when her father left. But in her room she found a magic mirror that said,

"Little Beauty, dry your eyes,
You've no need for tears and sighs.
Gaze into this looking glass,
And what you wish will come to pass."

This made Beauty feel more hopeful.

As the weeks passed, Beauty realised that the Beast wasn't really frightening. He was always kind to her, and in time she grew fond of him.

Then one day the Beast asked Beauty to marry him. Beauty had to say no. Although she liked him, she could never marry a Beast!

One morning, Beauty looked in her mirror and asked to see her father. She was shocked to see that he was ill.

When she asked the Beast if she could go home, he looked sad.

“I’ll come back as soon as I can,” Beauty promised.

The Beast gave her a ring. “Lay this on your table when you want to return,” he told her.

In an instant, Beauty was at home. And as soon as her father saw her, he began to get better.

The weeks passed swiftly. Then one night Beauty dreamed of the Beast. He was lying in the rose garden, weak and ill. He was starving himself to death because he couldn't bear to live without her.

When Beauty awoke, she knew what she must do. She laid her ring on the table and the next moment she found herself beside the poor Beast.

"Dear Beast," she said, "don't die. I *do* love you, and I *will* marry you!"

Suddenly there was a flash of light, and the garden was filled with music. Where the Beast had been, there stood a handsome young prince.

"Oh, Beauty, you've set me free," he said. "Long ago, a wicked fairy turned me into a Beast, and only the love of a beautiful woman could break the spell. You are the beautiful woman, Beauty!"

Beauty and the Prince were married amidst great joy, and Beauty's father came to live nearby. Together, they all lived happily ever after.